Copyright © 2004 by Nord-Süd Verlag AG, Gossau Zürich, Switzerland
First published in Switzerland under the title *Monstermädchen Mona*.
English translation copyright © 2004 by North-South Books Inc., New York

First published in the United States, Great Britain, Canada, Australia, and New Zealand in 2004
by North-South Books, an imprint of Nord-Süd Verlag AG, Gossau Zürich, Switzerland.
Distributed in the United States by North-South Books Inc., New York.

Library of Congress Cataloging-in-Publication Data is available.
A CIP catalogue record for this book is available from The British Library.
ISBN 0-7358-1945-9 (trade edition)
1 3 5 7 9 HC 10 8 6 4 2
ISBN 0-7358-1946-7 (library edition)
1 3 5 7 9 LE 10 8 6 4 2
Printed in Denmark

For more information about our books, and the authors and artists
who create them, visit our web site: www.northsouth.com

MONA
THE MONSTER GIRL

By Moritz Petz • Illustrated by Maja Dusíková

Translated by J. Alison James

North-South Books
New York • London

The night was slowly fading away. The first rays of daylight fell through a small attic window.

"Time for bed," called Mona's monster mother.

But Mona was afraid of the light. "What if there is a scary child hiding under my bed?" she said.

"Oh, Mona," said Mother, "there are no such things as children. They are only make-believe. And here, in our lovely, chilly attic, there certainly could never be any children."

Mona's monster mother tucked her in tightly. She gave Mona another good-day kiss. But when she left the room and shut the door, Mona was still afraid.

Mona peered anxiously from under the covers. What if children *did* exist? There might be children that Mama didn't even know about, children who would eat little monster girls. Right behind the curtain, weren't those eyes? Was that a noise from under her bed? Mona ducked under the blankets, trembling.

The bright sun warmed Mona's covers. Outside, the birds sang sweetly. Eventually Mona's eyes closed and she fell asleep.

Suddenly, she woke with a start. There! She heard it again! A loud, squeaky creaking. Mona froze as she saw the door in the floor slowly rise. A horrible little child's face glared out into the room. Another child was right behind the first.

"AAAAAH!" screamed Mona.

"EEEEEI!" screamed the children.

With a clunk, the trapdoor fell back against the wall. The horrible children disappeared.

At first, Mona didn't dare move. Finally she slipped out of bed and tiptoed to the open hole. Slowly, terrified, she looked over the edge.

There they were! Two children, a boy-child and a girl-child, were standing at the foot of the stairs. They saw her! They looked straight at her. Mona opened her mouth to scream . . .

. . . and got a face full of water. The boy-child had aimed his water pistol right at her. Mona was soaking wet. She started to sob.

Then she heard the wicked children start up the steps again. They were after her! Crying and shivering and dripping wet, Mona ran around looking for a place to hide. Just in time, she crouched under the table.

"The monster is crying!" said the girl-child, astonished.

The boy-child said, "I didn't mean to scare her."

Mona opened her eyes and looked up. The girl and the boy were right next to her. They looked worried.

"I'm very sorry I got you wet," the boy said.

Mona nodded slowly. She wiped the tears from her face. "It was kind of fun, actually," she said. "You see, I'm never allowed to get wet. My mother doesn't like me to be clean."

"Wow, I wish *my* mother were like that!" said the boy. "By the way, my name is Lenny."

"And I'm Maria," said the girl. So Mona introduced herself.

"Do you live here?" asked Maria. "In our attic?"

"I don't live in *your* attic!" Mona said. "You live in *my* cellar."

"How come we never see you?" Lenny asked. "Do you ever go outside?"

"Of course," said Mona. "I always play on the roof and in the trees, you know, games like Don't Touch the Ground, and Hide and Spook—but only at night."

"That sounds like fun!" said Maria.

So they ran outside to play a quick game right then.

It was the first time in her life that Mona had been outside in the middle of the day. The bright sun made it easy to find the two children's hiding places.

Then Maria and Lenny showed Mona their rooms. It was getting so late in the day, Mona could barely keep her eyes open, so she fell asleep in Maria's bed.

Suddenly, the children's mother burst into the bedroom. Mona awoke in a panic and sat bolt upright in bed.

"Maria," their mother said, "this room is a nightmare. Clean it up right away. Lenny, that goes for you, too."

She didn't even notice Mona.

The children were amazed. And Mona was baffled. She didn't understand why their mother had looked right through her.

"I hate cleaning my room," Maria sighed.

"What do you mean?" Mona cried. "I'm never allowed to clean my room! Would you let me do it? Please?"

So Mona picked up and sorted and put things away. Maria and Lenny laughed with delight, for Mona, like all monsters, had no idea where things were supposed to go in a child's room, so she put their toys away in some very unusual places.

"If *our* mother didn't see *you*," Maria said thoughtfully, "perhaps *your* mother won't be able to see *us* either."

They decided to find out. The three of them went to Mona's mother's room.

"Mona, you're awake," her mother said, surprised. "What are you doing up?"

She didn't see the two scary children. She didn't hear them either, even though they were both giggling.

"I just woke up and wanted to see where you were," Mona said, smiling. "I'll go back to bed now."

Mona really was sleepy, but she agreed to play one more game with her two new friends before she went to bed. At last, she went back up the attic stairs, tired to her toenails.

Lenny said, "I don't think it is so awful to have a monster in the attic."

Mona was insulted. "Of course it isn't awful to have me. I'm perfectly friendly. You two are the scary ones. But not anymore. I just didn't know that children could be so much fun."

Mona quietly shut the door in the floor She stretched
out happily in her bed. This time she didn't
hide under the quilt. She fell asleep in an
instant and didn't have a single daymare. She dreamed
of children, nice children, who were friendly and who
always wanted to play.

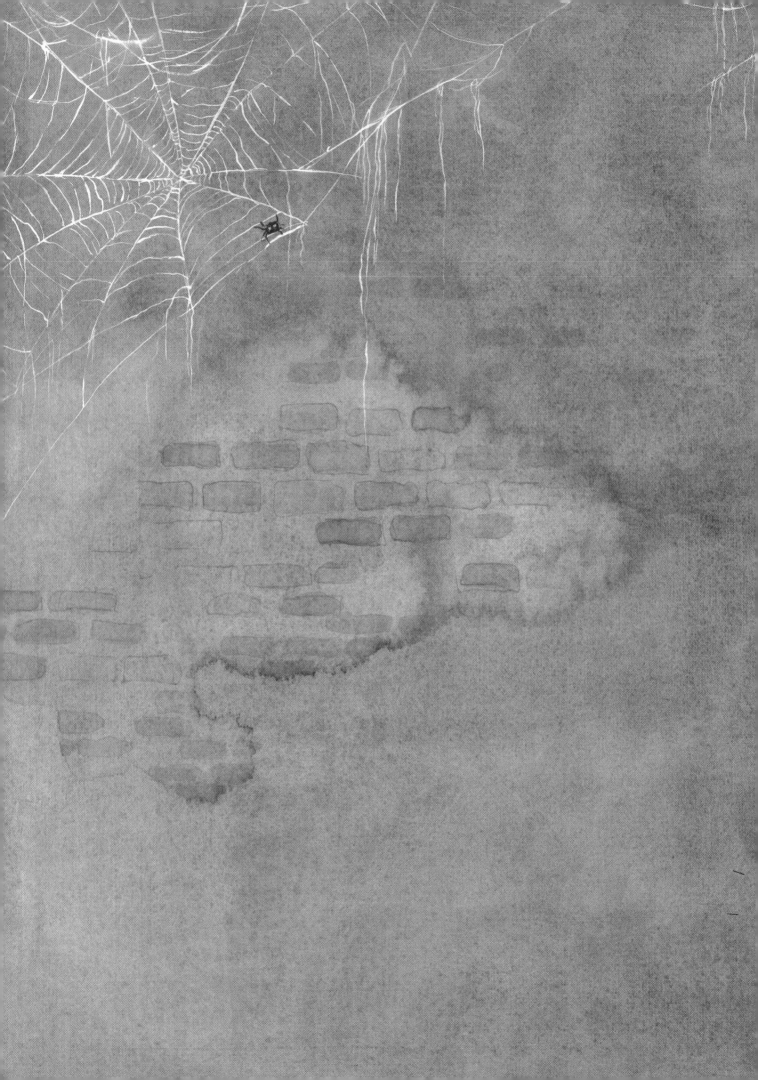